Caliche Dust
Foul Tips and Brief Summertime Loves

Joe Hardgrove

2nd Tier Publishing

Published by:
    2nd Tier Publishing
    501 Wimberley Oaks Dr
    Wimberley, TX 78676-4671, U.S.A.

All rights reserved. No part of this book may be reproduced or transmitted in any form or by any means, electronic or mechanical, including photocopying, recording or by any information storage and retrieval system without written permission from the author, except for the inclusion of brief quotations in a review.

Copyright © 2014 by Joe Hardgrove

ISBN 978-0-9862290-0-8

Illustrations by Faith Harrison
Book and cover design by Dan Gauthier

Acknowledgements

Besides thanking all the people whose personalities I "borrowed" for this book of short stories and poems, I must thank two people who aided in this publication.

First Mary Johnston Northern, who encouraged me to publish much of the work I've done in the past. Her encouragement and ideas were priceless. Another can't-do-without was my wife, Carolyn. Her guidance and cool demeanor, as well as her work on the computer, made this group of stories keepable and readable for many years for my children, grandchildren... and of course, you.

I must thank Dan Gauthier and 2nd Tier Publishing for the gentleness and flawless job that he has done in the editing and layout of this book.

CONTENTS

Acknowledgements   iii

About the Author   vii

Reflections and Foul Tips   1

Rocket in the Oklahoma Sky   11

Pay Back   14

Broken Bats   15

Two Roads Taken   17

Joaquin Jackson   23

Why a Friday Night Without Her   27

White Clouds   29

Roads and Rainstorms   30

Lunch Break   33

Austin City Limits   37

Soft Rugs, Sun Bathed Carousels, Cinnamon Rolls and Coffee Black   41

Everyone Needs Some Days Off   45

Sydney and Marsha   49

Paige Planchard   53

Caliche Dust   56

Keeping Quiet   59

Time Well Spent   65

Goodbye   69

About the Author

Joe Hardgrove has spent more than 50 years in the investment advisory business. Mr. Hardgrove has had a varied background: he was an English teacher, played professional baseball in the NY Giants organization and coached baseball and basketball at the college/university level. He was a technical writer/editor and played saxophone in a number of small groups. He graduated from Texas A&M University, and attended TCU and North Texas University for graduate work in a degree in English. He is a retired U.S. Naval Officer.

He has authored 4 other books—an isometric publication for women, *Trim Control*; a book of Christmas Eve short stories entitled *Birds of a Feather*; a memoir, *When September Comes*; and an economic and investment history of the late 20th century—*Connecting the Dots*.

Mr. Hardgrove now spends his time writing and acting as a director in a 50l(c)(3) donor advised charitable organization—Omega Foundation.

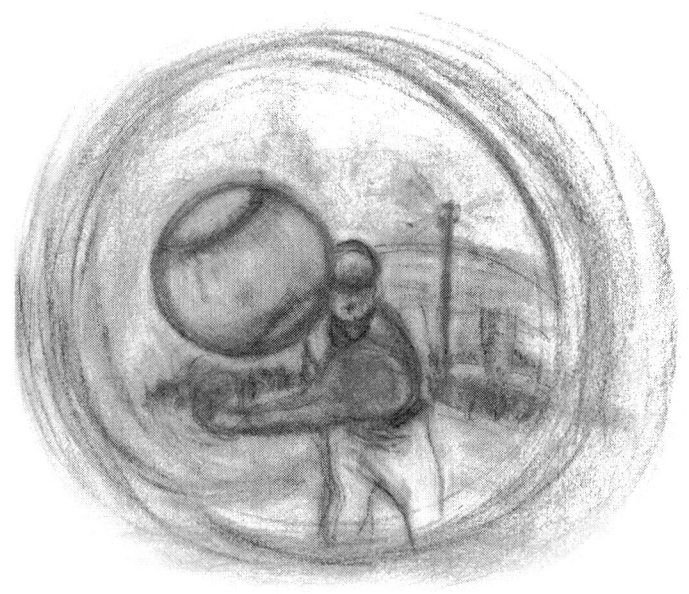

Reflections and Foul Tips

Ron watched the red Georgia clay moving under his feet beneath the converted Manor Bread truck, as 16 legs pushed against the hot loose dirt until the engine finally turned over. As the driver moved the gears into neutral and raced the worked-over engine, the remainder of the Class B Danville Giant baseball club hurried to board before the engine died again. Ron remembered they had not even changed the color of that truck since it was acquired from the bread company. They figured since the Giant's colors were black and orange, it would not be wise to waste the money on repainting the truck turned into a bus.

Somewhere out there through the pine trees, the deep green grass, Burma Shave signs, and at the end of a 3-hour bus ride was another ballpark with a bad dressing room they called a clubhouse; where only three showers existed and only two worked. These ballparks always had lights that were bad and this gave the veterans on the visitors' club a reason to reach for a pocketed flashlight, turn it on and point it at the lights and anybody else who was looking. This, of course, turned a full house of standing rednecks to boo the visitors. It was all in fun, at least for the fans.

And then there were the "Annies"—the ladies in A and AA ball. They'd many times go on the road when the team did. All pretty and ready to party, they were either older single college girls or handsome divorced ladies who attracted the baseball scouts and the coaching/manager fraternity.

If you remember the film *Bull Durham*, realize that in real life 40 to 50 years ago, the girls Ron knew didn't have the legs Susan Sarandon had in the movie.

This was the low minor leagues in the forties and fifties. You had your farm boys from Iowa; cane cutters from Puerto Rico; steel mill helpers from Pennsylvania and off season cops from Modesto. They all figured they would go to the Show by the time they were 21. All had signed at 16 or 17, except one pitcher from Kansas, who had gone to a Junior College one year before he had decided to sign for $2,000. The players, in those days, would either jell on their own, or were sent to Class D and finally found their way back to the hay baler on the farm at home.

The major problem was that damned old curve ball—that thing that has broken hearts from the sand lots to the big leagues for years, since some Demon with unusually short arms invented it. But there was always the guy on his way down who helped you with the grip of a slider or how to hide the nails in your bat when you broke your favorite Louisville Slugger; or maybe kept you from breaking curfew or screwing around with a too-young summer love.

In reality, it was a stupid way to make a living—chasing some damn dream of the *Bigs*. First year guy in the Bigs made $7,000 a year at the most. That's not much now, but I guess it was then; but hell, what if you get good? Some of those guys made $15,000 or $20,000. And man, they rode trains on road trips not beat up converted bread trucks. And they had trainers who'd rub the pitchers arm with a hot liquid they called "throw hard"; a clubhouse, and a guy who would shine your shoes and hand out dry towels. They even served food and had beer in the clubhouse. Yea, it took a lot of bad times in the bushes to get to the "good times." Which was nothing new to the ball players; they'd grown up that way. Most of them had no other choice. Some of the old timers

Reflections and Foul Tips

would spend 9 to 10 years in the minor leagues before making it. They were tough old guys who'd cut you up with their spikes in a slide at second and stick one in your ear if you had hit one out in your prior at-bat.

But when some kid from Mobile, who was as black as a widow's dream, hit one 418 feet and, as they say today was a, "walk-off home-run", it all seemed worth it. And Ron had known the elation of sneaking a sinker past a big four-hole hitter for a strike out. And then later getting away with a spitter; and as it sunk at the plate, the cola liquid flew everyplace and his catcher covered for him, cleaned the ball on his pants—then Ron figured he did the right thing by signing his name on that $100 a week. What else could he do: sell insurance, fix a broken water pipe, chop cotton, or rob some gas station that had a half empty cash register? Hell, he'd bought a new washing machine for his mama and he'd probably get her a car too, after season.

You can take that to the bank!

Speaking of cars: he'd gotten one when he was in class C in the Northern league. He bought it off a lot for $75. It was a 1948 Pontiac, a 2 door job. It had a big radio with a big aerial and was a two toned green and white. It had a few too many miles on it, but it was a beaut.

He headed to the ballpark that afternoon for batting practice and after a few blocks, he noticed it was tough to steer and he figured it out—all four tires were going flat. He pulled into a filling station as quick as he could, and put, God only knows how many pounds of air in those tires. He knew he'd be a little early for batting practice so he parked the car and headed toward the clubhouse.

About that time Eno, Willie and Orlando, walked up. They were Central Americans, talking Spanish and were admiring that new car. With the sun still bright, it shined even more that it did when he bought it off that lot not an hour earlier. They talked about how pretty it was in Spanish and English; especially the big radio and the tall aerial coming somewhere out of the trunk

Ron told them that he was crazy about the car but he had one problem: "My Aunt is having some heavy surgery back home in Kansas and I needed to send the money I spent on this car to her to help her with that operation." The threesome looked at each other and waited for the pitch that they didn't know was coming.

Caliche Dust

"And I've got to sell the thing to get some money back so I can send it to her." Well, he had cast the line out and now he waited see if he got a bite.

"How much do you want for the car?" Orlando asked, in pretty good Puerto Rican English. "Well, I paid around $120 for it, but I'll take $100 for the car." The three prospective buyers got together, speaking Spanish, discussing their holdings, finally went into their wallets, and collectively handed Ron $100 in ones and fives. Ron was mouthing a prayer that the tires would stay up at least long enough for them to get into the clubhouse and start batting practice...and a prayer asking for forgiveness for exaggerating the cost of the Pontiac. Hell, he didn't have the money to pay for tires and buy the car too.

Well, that night Ron was in short relief. He did pretty well, pitched three good innings and knew that he was going to have problems with the tires on the car that he just sold, so he asked "Salty" Parker, his manager, if it was OK, since he had already played and gotten his running done, if he could go ahead and leave. He said he didn't feel well.

"Salty" said, "Good game, yeah, go ahead." As he walked out through the parking lot he noticed, yes, the tires were about flat. He had no idea what Willie and the other two would say or what would happen, but he walked home as he usually did before he had the car—which he no longer owned—only faster.

The next day, the car buyers said nothing about the car except Ron noticed, that afternoon, that the car was in the parking lot and had 4 brand new tires on it. There was no complaint; the three simply ignored the situation.

Now fast forward to the sixties. By this time Ron had been out of baseball and the Army. He was traveling for a sporting goods company. Since he was out of baseball, and while going through Houston he noticed by the sports pages that the Giants (who had moved to San Francisco by that time) were playing an exhibition game against the Houston team. He thought it would be a good chance to see Orlando since he, and a couple more guys, had made it with the Giants and were becoming stars. He went to the hotel that he knew they would stay in, gave Orlando a call, and they agreed to meet and have a cup of coffee.

Orlando showed up flashy as ever with that big smile on his face and Ron was really happy to see him. They sat down, ordered some pie, had some coffee, and before long they talked about the old days in the minor leagues. Finally Ron asked Orlando, "Orlando, whatever happened to the car that I sold you, Willie and Eno?" Orlando then came back with a very surprising answer to Ron. "You know Ron, that car is a great car. We love it, we still use it, and we leave it in Florida and store it over the winter. We use it every spring to do our traveling in. It still has the same set of tires and it's been a lucky purchase for us. And for only $100 it was a real steal!"

"You can't beat a good well cared-for 1948 Pontiac—with a BIG RADIO!"

The aging and former pitcher thought of many other vignettes in the minor leagues that can only be fit into a scenario of a small town pure American classic culture. He decided that one day he would write about them all.

Once on a fairly short road trip, Ron, sitting next to Tony Taylor was joking around with Al Stieglass, the Giant catcher. Tony turned to Ron and asked him to read a letter he'd received from his home town in Columbia. Since Ron could read and speak a little "Spangluage" he saw it was written in English and Tony, at this stage, had trouble reading the American language.

A little bit about Tony: He was probably 18, his third year in pro ball. He'd signed at 16, was a fine young infielder and was the property of the New York Giants. The players in those days never thought it could be any other way. Like most other Central and South American athletes, as well as U. S. players, they were nobody of any consequences to the Giants. This was baseball's attitude until a courageous black player fought a lengthy legal war until the system agreed to let the players organize; thus now there is freedom and better benefits for the guys who swing the bats and throw the balls. As these things played out as the players union and selfish owners spent millions fighting each other. A sad time as threats of strikes, free agents and outsized bonuses to Big League players changed the game until the Old Time Fans hardly recognized it.

Anyway, as Ron began to read the letter, Tony began to sob. Ron was reading to Tony and as he blinked a tear out of his own eye, all he could think of was why in the hell would somebody write a letter and

Caliche Dust

tell an 18-year-old kid that his mother had died in a language he didn't understand or read.

But that was the nature of things in those days. The blacks and browns suffered in many ways like this. Like when they'd stop and the Southern café proprietors wouldn't serve them because they had blacks on the team. Everybody, all of them, always got their food inside, and then ate on the bus.

And Tony, that day he didn't eat.

These times helped baseball experience integration before the rest of the country. But don't kid yourself, the black and brown players were only accepted on the field based on their ability. Interestingly enough, the white guys didn't exactly go out drinking with the blacks and browns but you'd notice that the white Southern boys especially, carried over their respect for the minorities from the field to the streets. It wasn't the same, though, for the guys from the Northern and Eastern states. That's just how Ron watched it happen in the minor leagues in those days.

Ron remembered his first time as a starting pitcher, and his first encounter with a black guy. He was in the top of the ninth at home with a 3-2 lead with 2 out and men on 2nd and 3rd. A big left-handed hitter, with the Redding Indians hit a hard slider slicing for the left center field fence. His center fielder, Jesse Reagan, climbed the fence, made the catch to end the game. Ron grabbed Jesse out behind 2nd base and hugged him like a mad man.

It was the first time Ron had ever gotten close enough to shake hands with a black man, much less hug. Not so now. Jesse was Ron's pal. And it lasted for many years.

LATER ...

The trip to Longview was a pleasant one. And Ron, driving the rental car, saw some Hispanic and Black kids playing baseball in a green meadow that epitomized East Texas. He stopped to watch. Hell, he still could not get baseball flushed out of his system. He figured he wasn't old enough yet, so he fished out some chewing tobacco from the glove compartment, sat on the car's front fender and watched the kids playing a man's game.

No, not quite. He'd played ball in his 20s and 30s and he figured men playing baseball for a living was not a man's game. It would always be a kid's game. Being involved in the sporting equipment business just wasn't as good as playing, but he made a lot more money.

In another flash back he remembered Binghamton, New York. Freddie Osorio was pitching for the Giants against the Yankees farm team in a Class A packed ballpark in the mid 50s.

Pitching for the Yankee team was Jim Coats, a guy who was destined to go to the Big Leagues in the next couple of years. The guy threw damned hard. Probably in the mid 90s. Jim was from a place called Bulls Gap, Kentucky. He was about 6' 5", and as Ron noted, he threw bullets.

In those days there was no such thing as a designated hitter, and in about the third inning, Coats came up to bat and Osorio did a stupid thing. The Cuban right-hander, either purposely or accidentally, knocked Jim Coats down with a high hard fast ball. There were a lot of ooh's and aah's and most of them came from our dugout. We knew that if Coats was thrown at, that not only would he throw at Osorio, but he would make a choice of somebody on our ballclub to get plunked somewhere near their left ear.

Coats was steaming. Mike Turturo, our second baseman, called time out and went to the mound quickly, as did the entire Giants infield. They told Osorio, in Spanish and in English, that he was crazy as hell, because if he hit Coats everyone on the ballclub was in danger. In those days umpires didn't bother throwing a man out of a game for "accidentally" hitting another player.

Osorio said he understood, and everybody went back. The next pitch was a strike and the next one was a hard curve ball that Osorio didn't pull down enough, he lost control of it and it went right under Coats' chin. Coats was livid. He took about 5 or 6 steps toward Osorio with his bat cocked and the whole bench emptied to hold Coats back. The umpires kept it from being a fight. The umpires and Mike Turturo went to Coats during this time out and assured him that it was a mistake and Osorio wasn't throwing at him. Coats told them all what he thought of Osorio and that he would not forget the fact that he'd been thrown at.

The fact is that Coats was from Kentucky, in the south, and in 1956, Osorio might as well be from South Africa. For the next 6 innings Coats was unhittable and threw a 3-hit shutout; but the 9th inning

Caliche Dust

didn't end it for Coats or Osorio. When the game ended Coats was headed for the Giant's dugout, and if it hadn't been for Andy Relick, the Giants first baseman, Coats would have pulled Osorio's head off. Relick, however, talked some sense into Coats and he walked away accompanied by the manager of the Yankee ballclub.

The next day however, the picture changed. During batting practice Coats made some crack at Osorio, and of course Osorio popped back at Coats in Spanish. Coats couldn't speak or understand Spanish, but he was prepared for any problem or thing that the Cuban right hander might say or do.

He pulled a long-barreled handgun, a six shooter, from his warm-up jacket and waived it at Osorio!

Osorio started running towards centerfield and all that either team could do was stand frozen, especially after he pointed the pistol at Osorio and fired off two rounds. Every player on both ballclubs hit the dirt and Coats started chasing Osorio towards the centerfield fence. Finally someone on the Binghamton team yelled, "Don't worry. He's only got a cap pistol!" That did not deter Osorio one second. He reached the fence and somehow managed to climb the fence and disappear over a 360 foot sign board, which sported an advertising sign for an exercising workout studio and one extolling the benefits of a particular headache powder. Osorio couldn't have chosen a more ironic place to disappear behind the fence.

Everybody on both ball clubs was laughing. Even the managers and coaches thought it was one of the funniest things they'd ever seen. Naturally some of the officials at the ballclub came out, and somehow got the pistol away from Coats. But Coats was laughing more than anybody else on the field.

But what of Osorio? Osorio disappeared for the whole game. He never bothered to come to the dugout but as the bus was leaving the parking lot after the game, here comes Osorio banging his hand on the door, wanting to be allowed to enter the bus. When he came aboard, he was not prepared for the laughing and joking everyone on our club had for him. He delivered quite a speech in Spanish, gesturing with his hands and, according to some of the other Hispanic players, was swearing revenge on Coats.

Needless to say, for the third game the next night, the ballpark was packed with standing room only. Osorio stayed in the dugout and didn't even bother to go down to the bullpen. They let Coats coach first base and he got many cheers and many rounds of applause, as he tipped his hat to the home crowd numerous times.

Learning the Game

A favorite baseball story of mine centered in Johnstown, Pennsylvania—summer 1955. We'd lost the franchise in Wilkes Barre, Pennsylvania and had traveled ten days with all our belongings in cars, playing road games all along the way. It was during the great flood in the Leihigh Valley. The weather was hot...muggy, and this time was truly what the minor leagues in the 50s represented...tough times. Air conditioning? Don't ask.

Anyway, on our first night in Johnstown, I was called in to relieve in the seventh inning of the first game of a twilight doubleheader against the Redding Indians, a Cleveland farm team.

Facing a young kid—18 or 19—with two men on and the score tied, I threw a sidearm curve (he was left-handed—so am I) and got a strike.

The kid was back on his heels.

Next pitch: a fast ball at his chin...next came a hard slider. Strike—outside corner—back on his heels again. And after another inside fast ball, the swinging strike at a bad sidearm curve. Strike out!

We come in, score the winning run, and I get the win.

Later that night at a pizza/beer joint just off the street, I'm with my roommate—the before mentioned Mike Turturo. It was a hot night and we noticed a guy a few barstools over, by himself having a beer.

Mike says, "Hey, look. There's the guy you struck out tonight. Ask him down for a beer."

He was blond and young and when I asked him to move down the bar to us, he nodded, bringing his schooner with him. We only got five or six bucks a day in meal money in those days and most of that was always spent on beer. He was glad to sit with us and share some pizza.

Anyway, he came down and said that he knew that I was the one who struck him out, and he said, "Who's pitching tomorrow?" I replied, "Singleton." Jimmy Singleton, leading the league in strikeouts and ERA, was a side-arming left-hander.

Caliche Dust

The kid said to me, "Tell that SOB to throw me sidearm curve balls..."and I said, "You can't hit mine, how in hell will you hit his?"

And this cocky, blue eyed, crew cut kid said, "I know I can't hit 'em. But I'm going to the Big Leagues—I've got to learn to hit 'em..."

The kid?

ROGER MARIS

Rocket in the Oklahoma Sky

Max Peterson remembered the home run: the one in Lawton. The one with the bases full. He was in the first base coaches' box and said to himself, "This is why I jack with the game....this and only this." He had seen the ball go over the lights into the darkness, over the freeway. Took the team to the Youth World Series.

And he knew it meant more to his grandson than he showed at the time—God, the ball was hit!

It was even more important to Max because he never taught him to hit like that. He just taught him all those other things that made it possible for him to learn to hit like that. It was what Max was supposed to do. It was not until later when the kid figured the whole deal out—that you don't always win with techniques, you win with that something down deep which releases what ability one might have—that thing which cannot be taught. To acquire it, it must be observed and absorbed by the true recipient of that deep gift...sometimes it's passed through the genes, but in need of nurturing—loving—encouraging.

Caliche Dust

Whether it is watching others who drive themselves or just something a person figures out for himself,

...That's what makes it so valuable.

...You just don't know what it is

Max Peterson had never figured what this mystical "something" was—this thing that made one person possessing the same skill sets—whether it was doing something with a ball or a guitar or a numerical equation—that another could not do—even if each also had what appeared to be the same desire.

But whatever it was, it must be handled with care—possibly it's a perfect sculpture; maybe it's the strong fast hands on a Louisville Slugger's handle, or the smooth unthought-of—fluid delivery of a whistling curve ball, or maybe a precisely stated and logistically correct history lesson that can't be counted alone but must be delivered and smoothly passed to both the seasoned history student and the new first year freshman who'd never heard of T.E. Lawrence or King Faisal.

And don't forget the next vital step. It's one of Humility. The skill or talent or luck or whatever, it can be lost or maybe taken away for what reasons? Or no reason at all. Supernatural Sovereignty is a mysteriously blessed thing.

So the talent with the snapping slider at 91 MPH or the ability to explain to the lost visitor who stumbles into the church's sanctuary hurting, and hungry for someone to fill the hole that God had left there in his middle, which he has in deep sleep even dreamed, for just one relieving moment of cool nourishment.

And the driving athlete unable to figure why he makes the same mistakes over and over and gets to the point of even hypnosis, before he realizes the problem is not technique, but it's that thing called aloneness that promotes him to the bullpen of dejection until he somehow—someway sees the piece of the puzzle which is clear, that the proper mix of humility and courage and taking care to leave the credit to the observer, whatever the credit means.

Max had puzzled over these things for many years, which led to either success or failure, or at least to the perception of it.

But back to the ballpark! Max always has a habit of being a scatter shooter. You can't figure what it all means except one thing he knew.

Over and over again he'll not forget his grandson's shot into the Oklahoma night. It was another star on that starry night!

And that magic night he stopped and forgot about all the "whys" and "how's." So with a wide smile he drank of the cup of love and thanksgiving and put his thoughts to rest.

Pay Back

Sitting behind home plate,
The old man remembered his own fastball at sixteen.
He could not forget the exultation of the strikeout.

Watching the young pitcher he had taught
brought back all those highs he'd been through
not knowing at the time they were "highs."

And in the old days...
His generation never even considered, on the field,
a "high-five" rather than a handshake...
But this young man would pump his arm
and show things to the crowd and the victim he shouldn't have—
at the strikeout.

And in the third... on the first pitch...
his student took a fastball in the ribs...
The Old Man laughed to himself
and said, under his breath,
"Son, that's what you get."

Some things never change.

Turning from their television, somewhere out there,
One long gone old timer said to another old friend
"I love this game...
Let's play catch!"

Broken Bats
1955

He had seen the white half circle arc
play across the Texas blue sky and onto the
outfield green a million times.
When it was hit properly, the back spin
made little dents in the spring-splattered grass.

So the Ritual would begin again.
The crack of Louisville Sluggers...
the earthy smell of oiled leather...
the tightness of new baseballs...
the breathtaking view of the manicured outfield
which guarded the warning track and the green winter grass of the
infield—too soon to be replaced with the hardy Bermuda.
Yes, things still the same... when he once
discovered the truth of spring...
Start-Over Time...

He was an old man now and after
fifty-two-years of this, he figured
as he did each year, that the rebirth this time
was most splendid.

With painful fingers, which could no longer throw the curve ball,
he watched as usual from the bleachers as his
grandson moved with the exciting grace and handsome elegance
he once possessed.

And as he acknowledged the lonely truth of
the hourglass—
He once again started over.

Two Roads Taken

*I*t was one of those hot muggy days in North Texas that felt like Houston in the middle of the summer—one of those days when it's tough to breathe and even tougher heading to a funeral for an old friend you figured didn't have a lot of people to say goodbye.

Conrad Bennett and I were planning to have lunch on that day, but when I called him and told him I couldn't go because I had to go to a funeral he said, "That's interesting, because I'm going to a funeral too." When I asked him whose funeral he said, "Duck Anderton." Well, that was the same one I was going to, so we decided to go together. Later Conrad and his wife Laura picked me up in front of my building in a car that coincidently had just undergone an air conditioning loss. It was hot enough inside the car, but when you lowered the windows and got the breeze, it made it even worse, especially driving north up IH-35 toward the funeral home.

We pulled up into the sizzling concrete parking lot at the funeral home and we were about forty-five minutes early for the funeral. It was going to be a grave side service, so the three of us decided we would walk around to the site and at least try to find a spot in the shade.

Caliche Dust

While we walked, Conrad and I were discussing Duck Anderton's past. I had spent two or three summers with Duck and his buddy Eddie Chipman working at Texas Electric Service Company trimming trees in various parts of the city; played basketball against those two guys, Duck and Eddie, and had learned they were two pretty tough dudes. However, as the summer rolled on we became friends working on that tree trimming job.

It turned out that Eddie went off to college, got a degree in Business and went to work for a Fortune 500 company. It was in the early technology age and he moved up the sales ladder quite rapidly. It was in the days of the new communications systems, and Eddie was right on top and was a part of the cutting edge of that whole era. I was pretty sure that he had a truck load of stock and stock options. Eddie had retired at age 50 and owned a couple of condominiums in South Florida, was married and he and his wife lived on a boat most of their days in the Keys.

Meanwhile, Duck walked down a different path. Always willing to take a chance, he turned into a pretty good card player. He knew enough about sports to make some money gambling on football. While he was at this somewhat illegal occupation, he met quite a number of characters going through the same education process he was going through. Conrad and I agreed that Duck had never done anything extremely bad, he was getting his Business education in Texas rather than Nevada.

Duck ended up making book in a house over near Ridglea Country Club and doing quite well until the FBI picked him up and had all the evidence they needed to send him to the penitentiary for a few years. Matter of fact, he became pals with an old friend of mine, "Junior E", while they were incarcerated. "Junior E" had made a mistake in the DFW Airport by thinking the package a guy handed him in Miami was powdered sugar!

Unlike his buddy Eddie, Duck didn't really take good care of his body. After being released from prison at the age of around forty-five, and after getting back into his old business, he had a sudden heart attack and died. He was living in Corpus Christi at the time and his obituary showed up in the Fort Worth paper since the funeral was going to be local. I had turned to my wife when I read it and said, "I think

I'll go to Duck's funeral, he probably doesn't have a lot of friends here in Fort Worth." Conrad had felt the same since he had known Duck as long as I had, and Conrad had as many friends in that industry as Duck did.

The grounds of the cemetery were well taken care of. Tall and strong oak trees shaded much of the burial places of many generations of North side citizens. It was a rather old cemetery but based on what we saw they kept pretty busy. In due respect to Duck, nothing was ever mentioned at the funeral whether Duck had made a religious conversion or not. It was an easy task to pray that he had.

Anyway, we finally reached the shade over by the gravesite and noticed a number of older people walking up toward the tent that covered the site. Most of the men had on suits, although the weather was beastly and many of those jackets looked like they had been hanging in a closet on wire hangers and still carried the dust around the shoulders. They probably had not been used since the last funeral. Many of the men wore "leisure suits", the garb du jour of the early 70s in Fort Worth, Texas. The fact is though; we were now in the 21st century.

There were some ladies too, and quite frankly, Conrad and I had recognized some of them; however, their faces were not as we remembered seeing over the years in bars and clubs around town. Most of the people approaching the gravesite gave the appearance they'd just come from a wake at a local North Side bar, which was definitely a fact. Most of the mourners appeared to be in their sixties, maybe early seventies. Conrad and I decided that that was just the age they looked. They were really in their early to mid-fifties.

As Conrad said, "That booze does a job on you especially when you're out in the sunshine, at an old buddy's funeral, and it's about 102 degrees."

The service began and it turned out that the preacher who was handling the funeral was a young Baptist boy whom we discovered later was a product, and still enrolled, in the Baptist Theological Seminary here in Fort Worth. He had a hand held mic and encouraged the crowd to move as close as they could to the tent. Of course the seats in the tent were already filled, so the crowd, along with Conrad, Laura and me, stood outside not being able to escape the sun which seemed to have been conjuring up a hot message for all of us.

Caliche Dust

The music started. It was a young guy with a guitar and a harmonica hooked up to a gizmo on the guitar. He sang and played some blues tunes only they weren't blues; they were church songs in a blues key which I enjoyed tremendously. I felt like we were getting our money's worth because we did come to a funeral. We expected to hear some religious music, but never dreamed that we would hear religious music played like we always hoped it would be played. It made both Conrad and me think about plans for our own funeral.

When the music stopped the preacher started. He had obviously just taken an Evangelizing class at the Seminary. Let me say this in the beginning, I'd been to these types of funerals before, but Conrad was destined to be puzzled. First there was the music, which he enjoyed, and then we decided that anybody who had ever been primed to preach to a bunch of people who'd spent all morning in a bar drinking, and many who had probably done some time in the "pen," as Duck had done. This young preacher got the blue ribbon.

This kid was ready. As I watched the crowd, I saw beads of sweat roll down foreheads. The young Baptist preacher was letting them have it with fire and brimstone he learned in school. He talked about Hell just like he had been there and knew all about it including naming some local characters he figured were there right now. He was preaching pretty strong—pointing his finger at the crowd as they moved from one leg to another. I'd never seen a crew listen to a sermon that was perspiring like this gang was. The young preacher obviously knew his congregation. When added to the heat of that day, it became a memorable event. The young preacher gave an altar call and instead of answering the call they just shuffled from one foot to the other.

Well, finally the sermon ended and we went to *Amazing Grace* and the long haired young man on the guitar gave Mr. Anderton another good blues song before the Baptist preacher started his last goodbye prayer. The mourners at the funeral wondered, as did Conrad and I, how long the prayer was going to last.

One guy flat passed out before the final *Amen*. Some peopled figured that God was right there knocking people to their knees! One of the attendees was in a wheel chair. He had lost a leg somewhere along the line, and he had a good friend who was pushing him across the grassy property, getting in a position to go back to the parking lot when the prayer ended. When the funeral was finally over they broke up and obviously most of the crowd were headed back to their cars to go to a more comfortable location, which would be that same North Side bar they'd left. I did notice that the guy in the wheel chair was flipped out of his chair and it took about four of his pals to get him back in. Then one of the former bartending beauties took charge and headed toward wherever they were parked. This was quite a sendoff for Duck.

A few months later, Conrad and I were having a cup of coffee and talking about the funeral when he looked at me and said, "Joe, did you remember to smile?" and I said, "What are you talking about, Conrad?" He said, "Well, when we were out there at the funeral I hope you were smiling as much as you could because the FBI was in the woods taking pictures of everyone at the funeral."

We got a big laugh out of that and we agreed: both Conrad and I were glad we had given up some of the activities that we had been involved in as young men. Life is much better when you at least try to walk a straight path.

Interesting how two guys who grew up going to the same school, living in the same neighborhood, as Duck and Eddie, had each found a different path to walk. Choosing a road to travel is always left up to the traveler. Most of us have had both good and bad advice. Both positive and negative paths are not chosen in one day. Listening to good directions usually gets us to a fullfilled future. A few steps in the wrong direction can change the whole picture.

So rest in peace, Duck Anderton. Too bad Eddie couldn't be here to bid you goodbye.

This story is dedicated to Laura Bennett, in honor of Conrad, her husband, my great friend, who passed away in 2012.

Joaquin Jackson

I gave Leo Willett a compendium of pictures from *Texas Monthly* as a retirement gift this weekend. On the cover was a picture of a now-retired Texas Ranger–Joaquin Jackson. Married to Shirley Jackson, a former C&W singer, Joaquin found Johnny Rodriguiz, more notable than Shirley, as a recording star. All of them could have been found in the mid 70s in Uvalde, Texas. Joaquin being the "Ranger in charge" of God knows how many counties.

In the mid 70s Jimmy Williams and I, both single or at least semi that way, trekked from San Antonio to Uvalde in my '72 Pontiac to visit Gordon Sutton, entrepreneur—land salesman and son of onehellof a wealthy doctor in San Antonio. I'd known Gordon for years and written a sales book for him and several of his "land salesmen" touting five acre tracts in the Hill Country.

Anyway Williams and I and Gordon started a fire 30 yards from the ranch house Gordon called home on the acreage he was selling and by the time darkness folded us in, Gordon decided to turn on the Christmas lights strung above us to light the way to the "dirt cheap tracts" he sold.

Caliche Dust

There we were sharing Cutty Sark and water. The ice chest was in the back of Gordon's Lincoln. The black car was standing like a civilized rebel in the dark night juxtaposed against the shrub brush and dead trees that Gordon had wasted the beauty of the land with. No one wants to buy land that's got shrub brush and stumps on it. So Gordon had burned any sign of them.

And then about 9:00 p.m. and before we started the steaks over the fire, we saw the headlights twisting up the road to the house and now seeing the fire, the beams turned south and came at us. The car, with black sidewalls, was strictly government issued—stopping now, released its driver—Mr. Joaquin Jackson, a by-God Texas Ranger that nobody could argue with. He was 6'5" and wore the silver star that the Rangers have worn for 100 years.

Dressed in jeans and a tight-fitting short denim jacket, Joaquin came to the fire and Gordon greeted him with great exuberance.

Gordon had told us that he always had to find ways to get Joaquin hip pocket money without hurting their relationship. Nothing big. Just walking around money.

Joaquin wore a Resistol hat with a snakeskin band and when he came to the fire we offered him a drink, smelling of Aramis (the cologne de jour of the 70s) he politely refused since, he said, that later that night in that deep Texas Ranger voice, "I've got to meet an informer."

Gordon wasted no time. "Joaquin, I'll give you $50 if you can shoot out one of the lights I've got strung from here to the house."

Joaquin, embarrassed, shuffled his boots, but finally moved to the Lincoln's side, reached under his jacket (it looked like the kind General Eisenhower wore in the war—an "Ike" jacket) and from his back belt he drew a Colt .45. I remember that the barrel looked short; maybe because his hands were so big. Anyway, he leaned against that shining black Lincoln and blew three lights away with four rounds. We said, "Great shooting," and Gordon gave Joaquin two $50s. Joaquin tried to decline but Gordon insisted, and taking advantage of the opening, asked Joaquin to show Jimmy and Joe real fire power. Showing that "Eastwood smile," the Ranger opened his trunk and produced an automatic rifle and proceeded to absolutely destroy a dead tree nearby. I discovered later that it was an armorlite AR-18 assault rifle. And as

Joaquin said, "the AR-18 is a reliable American made little metal maelstrom. The gun, quite simply, is a very bad boy."

We wanted Joaquin to stay, have some beer and steak, and tell us some stories. We knew he could have kept us till dawn. But he could not; had to go.

So we cooked our steaks, listened to Willie on the Lincoln's tape deck and finished the quart we'd only started earlier. I guess when you're 40 and semi-single, you don't check the time of day till tomorrow comes.

The next morning we slid into the Lincoln and were bound for the Ramada Inn for breakfast when Gordon glanced in his rearview and said, "Joaquin just picked us up."

I was excited since I knew a breakfast with Joaquin would produce a story or two. Sure enough he joined us and as we drank our first coffee I asked, "Joaquin, did you make contact with your informant?"

He was freshly shaved, clean and smelled once again of the Aramis.

"No," he said. "He didn't show." But at 2:30 I was driving down Main when this guy crossed in front of me. I recognized him as the same kid Johnny Rodriguez had pointed out who tried to give him some marijuana one night at a party in San Antonio. When Johnny told me that I found the kid and I told him to get the hell out of Uvalde and never come back to my county. And here he was right in my headlights—like a deer on the highway.

"I stopped him and he gave me some smart assed answer as to why he was here. I took him in."

"He called his Daddy on the phone and you know what he told his Daddy? Told him I'd grabbed him and hit his head on my car bumper. What happened was, the kid was stoned, fell down and bumped his head on my car. Can you believe that? I knew there was something wrong with the boy because he was obviously a liar. After I talked to his daddy, the boy decided he'd move to California."

"Hey, Gordon, pass the strawberry preserves. Can't believe that kid—lying to his Daddy that way. I just love strawberry preserves on hot biscuits. If I ate like this everyday, I'd weigh 300 pounds."

June 2011

Joaquin wrote a memoir in the mid 2000s, *One Ranger*. I sent him a copy of this story. He thanked me and sent me an autographed copy of his book.

Caliche Dust

Our company began handling the management of the Texas Ranger Endowment Fund in 2009 and after meeting a number of Rangers, I learned two things: First, "Don't mess with a Ranger." Second, "Don't mess with a Ranger."

Joaquin is happily retired in Alpine.

Why a Friday Night Without Her?

He was perhaps 61...or who knows?
He was balding, black, gray bearded,
Head shining like tea ivory.

He played bass...with blue/black
Suede shoes and tux
Which I loved... he was not
French-cuffed...

His bass was also tea colored
(Never saw one like it).
He played his solo (Body & Soul)
On the high notes.
He embraced the bass strings
Like you make love... soft tender fingers

He had a day job...I figured.
But if he had had
His way –
He would say, "I quit!"
His collar was loose...so was his tie.

Three drinks...I'm still here. Why?
I guessed at his children/grandchildren.
Had he showed them the moves?
Did they know he played?
Had they ever heard him?
Did they come see/hear him play like some
Ballplayers' kids do?

He had not yet known the pain
He was not aware of the pain
That he would know that
Not being able to play his
Music would bring...
The pain in his fingers would be
Nothing... compared to that.

Would he eventually use the bow?
I hope not—And now...
I watch his eyes close...
Behind the blue tinted shades. And
This time it was "Lover Man"...

There are better hotel bar combos
And the piano guy ran the deal,
But it was the bass guy
Who owned me that night.

And as I studied his sounds,
I looked briefly at the
Sign above his head.
The red one...It said
Exit

And then it was over.
I'd been over served
And
With the last "A" chord, by the piano,
I remembered
Why I was here.
There's nothing wrong
With being over served.
What else would a guy do
After she has whispered the final
Goodbye

White Clouds

White clouds looking like iced
Corn rows...or cotton rows, maybe—
Or maybe icicles hanging from a coke sign slowly melting
Somewhere between New York and Fort Worth.

And the sun dresses the clouds that
Protect the blue of nothingness that
Covers Lexington, Kentucky, or some
Other place he'd passed over before—

With her...and without her...

Whether they were side by side—or 2,000 miles apart

With a chain of consistency—Loving him—from the very first...

And that dusty late afternoon
Following drinks and quiet talk
When in the warm twilight she smiled
That disabling flash and they kissed

In the car outside
Casa Del Sol.

She smelled the coming West Texas rainstorm,
and stepped into her car outside the club.
And recognizing the heat of sticky asphalt
and rain coming almost unannounced—he drove slowly
So she'd not miss the turn—
Following him
And suddenly like a gunfighter in the old days of black and white movies
Lightening, thunder and rain swept them through the steamy afternoon.
Then in a timeless dash they
Broke for the apartment's door—
And the rain came just as they both hoped it would.

Roads and Rainstorms
1954

One minute they were
Hearing the old songs
Speaking thru the sax section
And Ellington was back—
Alive on the Mall—

First the dust—
Then the wind hustled
A hundred paper cups
And yellowed napkins
Before the rain hit
Like gravel spun beneath
Cycle wheels while
The listeners folded their blown blankets.

They ran to the blue
Shelter parked next
To the blowing grass
Which allowed the
Rain to hurt it...
Not them.

And now later.
The room welcomed them—
Holding both in its
Shadows like a dream
You have, when quicksand
Becomes heavy—even pulling
Them closer than the rain had done—
Outside—safe now...

The music said the things
They both thought...
And Ellington melded into Sinatra...

And while they danced, he
Recalled her hair, and hands and body
In those other days and how
He would not have believed
If someone had told him
Then he could still love her...
They danced their private
Slow dance—
Saying nothing.
As he often said, their
Silence said more than
They dared speak of...
From where they started—
And the years...
The damned quick years—
And now, streaking by like
A hurried-up-movie—
Only stopping at those times
When he
Could find time to watch—
Capture—develop...
That's when the movie made
Him always think
Of another road.

Lunch Break

He paid little attention to the staring Hispanic girl sitting in a side booth with her co-worker friend.

Thus, he was surprised to hear what his new acquaintance said:

"She either thinks she knows you or wants to know you."

Glancing at the girl in the booth he chuckled and wondered if this new lady was psychic or simply commenting.

"What do you mean?"

"You know what I mean."

Just then his mind caught the sound of quiet music—jazz, he remembered, and the music blended into her laughter. Now turning and sensing her perception, he noticed her eyes.

He immediately recalled polished stones he'd seen in some shop in South America—H Stern, he remembered. They were

Caliche Dust

reflecting the autumn Brazilian sunlight streaming through the jeweler's window at an angle which he would remember forever.

There were questions marks and he began to wonder what suddenly happened to cause her to make such a rash statement to a guy she had only just met.

She quickly got up and walked behind a counter and just glancing, smiled a sudden flash that said:

"What the hell has just happened to me?"

He'd walked this road before: One, two more encounters, long lunches, drinks, the Slow Dance and ...

Not this time kid. There were too many bumps in that highway—and pot holes and shaken dreams, but he knew that this time the things he'd surely break would take longer to heal and...just forget it.

Are you kidding? How do you dismiss unforgettable green eyes and a mind that was so quick to recognize the right signs?

So time passed, and weeks later once more he walked the long Vacancy signed wide sidewalk (was this New York?) and into the café and now again the music... But other friends of hers, as if they had heard the music fading, all went their way to do whatever they had to do. But he had nothing to do so they sat together and once again the quiet music started and he changed stations in his mind, since he heard Slow Dance music rather than the soft jazz, which he realized fit her so well.

So they talked and again he saw those ice green eyes that were trimmed with a fleck of brown that matched her hair ... This time, when he left she joined him but only to the door and they quickly kissed and they were both gone.

He would review this landscape a dozen times in the idle months that followed. And finally he saw her again at another, different café. This time the food was Tex-Mex and she wore heels and fitted slacks, and there was that same sound of a soft sounding horn playing that warm jazz and he did not remember

Lunch Break

her being this tall or having such long legs. The music changed to Slow Dance and finally as the check came, they walked to the door, they kissed again, and this time he said goodbye forever.

But this time he walked away through unexpected rain. It was one of those times when you've walked away and wondered why.

austin City Limits

It was a black Chrysler. Clean.
Not tired from the 90-mile ride and just filled up with ethyl gas at 39-cents a gallon.

She, waiting on the second floor for the fire escape to be pulled down so she'd not to have to check out of the dorm; she'd return the same way. She'd not have to make up some story that gave her another hour with him. She inched close to him in the big car and glancing down, he noticed the hose captured by the black garter belt.

But now the Chrysler rolled north on Hwy-81 from the escaping sounds of the stadium crowd already half bombed. And they hadn't even had the coin flip yet.

He knew the joint well. Gravel and asphalt—sticky still—the South Texas sun and too early for the breeze off the lake, which along with her pleated navy skirt and smooth—as—hell cashmere sweater set, made him breathe the hot wind and be unable to avoid the thinking of how all the other girls loved football and she didn't.

Caliche Dust

So they stepped into their Saturday Afternoon Home where the well watered air conditioners welcomed them with the familiar smell of cigarette smoke and what he knew was Pearl beer.

Sometimes you're lucky to have lighting just like it always was at the other places he'd been with her. He looked at her face and remembered the time they stopped and walked into the salt water of the Gulf of Mexico and he suddenly saw her smile and her eyes reflected the moon's sad soft glow. And now once more that same knot in this throat came that touched him that night in Corpus Christi.

The club was not busy, maybe two, three others who could care less about football—

The ash trays, he remembered, were large and heavy and stamped with the name of some beer company.

They found a quiet dark booth and ordered drinks. After the tired waitress poured two J&Bs, he eased toward the juke box and found the De Castro Sisters waiting to sing to them "Teach Me Tonight" and so they danced. It was, as always, a slow dance and the cashmere sweater was smooth, soft to his hand. The pleated skirt worked well with the De Castro Sisters—and he thought of the flash of leg and her closeness initiated thoughts of old times in the Hill Country.

They stayed on the floor—someone played "Spring is Here" next and the magic that started last June continued until they both stopped, and leaning against the table, kissed, as the scotch started its work...and they kissed again.

In spite of the warmth of the dance floor, and after three scotches, suddenly she spoke of last summer when they ate cabrito under a mesquite tree right out on the flat prairie land—sharing rum and coke as they, and the other cowboys, laughed a lot—but now right there in the club, he saw in her eyes what was coming and she watched him turn away as the waitress passed—the old arguments and disagreements had taken their toll. Like turning off a light, and before she spoke he knew...

He sensed it. He figured she'd start it again—why do things change from August to November in such a vast, sad thinking way?

He knew suddenly that they were there—at another road block—and the Cold commenced—and after serious discourse—she just wouldn't leave it alone—Were they all like that?... Why did these things need ending? He'd always been unable to write meaningful last verse lyrics... He was simply not ready. He was not ready for kids and picket fences and PTAs. So once again he fished the Chrysler keys from his jacket pocket and said: "Time to go."

And then they left. Just like that.

Hell, it was time anyway—the big problem were those brown eyes turning into deep pools of tears and he remembering that old song by Sinatra, "I'll Be Seeing You in All the Old Familiar Places." And so as they had done the times before, they "kicked the can down the road," both saying they'd call...tomorrow."

Hell, he was already 21.

Now rolling back into the dim alley he helped her out of the car and into the heat behind the dorm. And she stepped up to the first fire escape stair; they kissed again, and he wondered if it would be the last. There just wasn't time. The things she wanted—not yet, maybe never.

He lowered the front windows on the big Chrysler and moved rapidly through the traffic toward the stadium. Hell, the game was probably over by now. He'd pick up his buddies and then he knew they'd want to talk about the game. It didn't matter to him, as long as there was plenty of Scotch for sale.

Later that night he would think of her...and called her—just to be sure she got back to her room OK.

After he hung up, he said aloud: "Wonder how far down the road I can kick that can?"

Soft Rugs, Sun Bathed Carousels, Cinnamon Rolls and Coffee Black

She had sent him a review of Dave Brubeck Carnegie Hall
And although he didn't immediately read it he
Noted a picture of Paul Desmond in the Times layout and
It plunged him back through the smoking past
To those nights they had sat and drank the scotch
And lounged in the love that poor skinny Paul (that's what
 Bevo had called him)
Had melded them in, that night in Dallas on the hard-
 wood floor and
He remembered the light from the shaded lamp
Made the rug look much softer.

And then came Chet and that strong horn
And the weak, clear sounding lyric he had before
Drugs and the heartbreaking rides in those cars
Seeming like Lawrence of Arabia

Caliche Dust

Having a death wish that protected him from his dreams
    coming true.

This, of course, took him back to her place,
Many years later listening to the rain blowing from the
    dark tall trees onto the glassed shield.
They did the close dance to Bennett singing Sinatra
And realizing that this record would always be his.
And then the carousel where he surprised her seen from a
    2-lane short bridge.
And the car as they drove into the park over a treed ridge
In just perfect weather.
He had forgotten whether they had ridden the carousel or not.
It did not matter.
He realized these times with her had been a fitting time.

Probably the memory so clear was that day they stood on
    the Hudson hillside
And leaned against the clapboard house and kissed...
The afternoon sun revealed paint starved wooden windows
As they watched the late fall river move as easily as his
    thoughts of the years that had passed.

On the train finally he hoped that she too would recall
    those moments
And flash herself back to Highland Park and the wooden
    floor.
And once again Bruebeck/Desmond playing "Lover" in
    ¾ time

    Finally he moved to the big Lincoln and stopped at the rail station's parking lot's gate. He waved good bye to disappearing sad eyes protected by that silver colored tube which reminded him of a lonely caterpillar making its escape from sad melancholy saxophone sounds. He could not remember the cue and which exit to take. Suddenly that old familiar choking came to his chest as he turned off the car's CD-player. He wondered if she'd had the same "goodbye" thoughts that he had.
    On his way to the airport, his cell phone buzzed. And he knew. He didn't bother to answer. He'd tried to rub the fog from his eyes, but

Soft Rugs, Sun Bathed Carousels, Cinnamon Rolls and Coffee Black

he couldn't reach his handkerchief. Now there was no turning back. Things just would not fit. He saw that now—not a timely choice.

The Lincoln's FM-radio played an often remembered song, "Gone With The Wind":

And they were both gone as easily as the wind was. Only they did not realize it.

To the airport he soared back in memory to the side street café where they had sipped coffee and spoke of those earlier days and both remembered how many years and miles had eased by—just like the easy stream of water he watched today as he slowed the Lincoln before entering a covered bridge.

He'd had problems with the situation for too long. Habit had overtaken them both. Once he made a getaway to Italy. Even in the light of the swinging Sicilian town, with women he was certain his pals would kill for; she had stumbled through his mind. She had said before he'd left for Europe that she'd believed the mistake they'd made was not getting married when they had been younger—before careers, deadlines, writers block, and smooth Kentucky Bourbon with birthdays that ended with too many large double-digit numbers.

The road had been tough for them both. He was a satisfactory, independent free-lance photographer and he'd shot any event the magazine (travel publication) called him to cover. Boring.

Hell, she'd once told him he sometimes wrote poetry that made her cry; but looking back he had tried to make pictures like he could write. Good profession, wrong job.

She practiced medicine until she became tired of the paperwork and government rules. So she sold the practice, moved to Florida, worked a while in an emergency room in Tampa, and finally bought a boat and lived on it.

She'd called him from Florida and he'd met her in Atlanta. They both had hoped the time apart could help them solve some problems about their relationship, which always came up when they were together too long. Maybe, he thought, the fact that they were much older would help them go back to a more stable time in their lives. No deal. Turns out they basically had exhausted all the things they used to talk about. Neither had desire for sex, and after a rather long lunch, she was ready to go back to her boat.

Caliche Dust

And driving himself to the airport, as the miles passed by, he suddenly saw the dawning of the truth. Damn! He was still alone and single after a bad marriage and a two year "hook up." No matter how he wrote it, or thought it, it was too late. He knew what happened to once fresh fruit when left out too long.

Then the cell phone rang. He turned it off. Turned the car's CD-player back on and now he heard the song again. He smiled and turned the volume up. "Gone With the Wind."

And the caller had hung up—for the last time.

Meanwhile, back at that side street coffee shop, another couple sat and shared a cinnamon roll with their coffee. After a quiet joint exchange of conversation, and before he could make the suggestion that they try again, the woman looked across the booth and said, "Goodbye." It made things so simple. He smelled the coming rain and knew what the wind would do. So he responded with a nod barely noticeable.

Everyone Needs Some Days Off

This tale was to begin in one town, Wilkes-Barre, Pennsylvania and end in another, Johnstown, Pennsylvania.

It started with a picnic in the Poconos with Mike Turturo and his girlfriend, Shirkey. Mike was my baseball roommate and teammate in the minor leagues in the 50s. My girl was Mary Greenwald. She was German-Jewish and lovely and naive and bright and open, and laughed with such a sound as to make you wish that baseball hadn't become so important to you and that maybe you had a trade or something that gave you nights off...but not today. Today was an off day and Mike and I drove from Johnstown to pick up Mary and Shirkey.

We changed to Shirkey's 1955 Black Chevy and moved through the clear Pennsylvania morning, smooth and easy in the new car. Only I should stop, she said, at the bicycle shop and drop off the shoe box sitting in the front seat between me and lovely Mary—cool and neat in a cotton sundress. I slid the Chevy into a loading zone in front of the wooden building. Then I looked in the box. There was cash—a hell of a lot of it. Not ones... $100s... Shirkey says, "Don't worry, its

Caliche Dust

yesterdays baseball money. Billo always wants it before noon." I looked at my watch. 11:35.

OK, now you want to know about Shirkey: Older, much older than she appeared, totally in love with Mike—and Mike, much younger, Italian, and Bostonian. Billo Walker: he controlled it all—gambling, prostitution and the joints on Lake Dallas: clubs, hotels, boats and their owners.

How a guy named Walker did it, I do not know. Maybe he changed his name.

That summer Shirkey would call at all hours to our room in Johnstown and Mike would make notes. Turned out it was horses, and he always won. Later when he told me I was his "front" as his roommate, it hurt for awhile, but I loved the guy. He left Johnstown after the season, rich; since the horses always did what Shirkey told Mike that Billo told the horses to do. We ended that day at Lake Dallas after the drop of the baseball money.

We changed and sat on the wooden deck on that perfect sunny day. We swam, at least Mary and I did, while Mike, and Shirkey talked and smoked and drank: Shirkey, with the Bombay and Mike, as usual, beer. It was like the sun did all those things that it was designed to do... in summer...on "off days"...when you had time and you were young and you were lying on the dock with someone you could fall in love with, stand up, walk to the dock's edge, leaving her to split the clean, cold Pennsylvania mountain water, shivering, and then back to dry and talk of next month, next year. I'd learned that it was always the future they thought of...

And later that night it was Shirkey at a quiet Italian place really older than I could imagine—began with the Scotch—and when she looked at Mary, she had almost cried with the thought of Mary's youth... leaning across the candle lit booth, and realizing...deciding that not only was it over with Mike, but—even at 45—deciding it was too late. Now, a different person...glaring at my Mary G. and not being able to go back...hell, not wanting to...and Mike holding her, with me not knowing what to do...the mob girl blurted cruelly that Mary's father wasn't a "technician," but really worked for Billo on the slots—repair work. She left nothing out to Mary...all the years her father had left out...and me...God, all I could see was the tears rising now in Mary G's eyes, with the terrible thought that she'd really never known her father, who had been rejected by his Jewish family since he had married the fine blond German girl he'd met—somewhere in his youth.

And the whole thing hurt Mike, which of course hurt me, since I'd never had a brother. And that night it all ended... I, in Shirkey's '55 Chevy, took Mary home after dropping Mike at Shirkey's.

Before the season was over in Johnstown, I answered the phone one night and after letting me listen to the Irish tenor at a club in Denver where she was drinking, Shirkey promised me that she'd get me a '55 at rock bottom—since she owned a guy in Detroit. And later, after season, I called Shirkey and she said she was sorry, but her guy in Detroit had left town and there was nothing she could do...which did not disappoint me, since at 22 I was well equipped to be taught another lesson.

The last time I saw Mary, I was back at Lake Dallas waiting for a bus and one passed...only slowed...did not stop. Mary was by the window and she looked out at me...and then turned away.

At Christmas time that year, I called Mike in Massachusetts. We talked of spring training and baseball. He'd gotten over Shirkey. Why not? New cars, stereos, and expensive watches cover a lot of love lost.

I called Mary a couple of times...left word and my number in Texas...but I never heard from her again.

And on cool, clear summer days, when the sun is just right, I think often of Lake Dallas and Mary.

Sydney and Marsha

Someone always asks about Sydney! Talk about a dream team. Marsha and Sydney were high school age (in those days, nobody worried about age). Sydney played piano. God, could this child/woman play piano! He had met them when he was a freshman at the university. They lived in the small college town and came to the club where he worked as a backup musician.

"Hum a few bars for me." That's what she'd say and when he did, she'd play those 50s songs in any key he wanted. So he, the college sophomore at 19 or 20 was picked by his musician friends to date Sydney, since he was the youngest, and played tenor sax...and Marsha, Sydney's sister, a beautiful 18-year-old who could sing the great American song book as if she had written the tunes. She was Peggy Lee and June Christy all in one and had a vulnerability and sadness about her that was heartbreakingly sweet when she sang with dance bands or with Sydney, the tenor sax; Rodney's uke and Jimmy Green on guitar with Garrison Ellis on trumpet. Ellis lived "across the tracks" and usually played that beat up horn with bruised and often bloody lips...he didn't have enemies; he just had a quick temper and couldn't handle it.

Caliche Dust

Those nights after hours they mixed the crisp fall and blues in F with songs Sydney would create...and Marsha would sing: My, could she sing! You see, the sax player's deal was to keep Sydney at the piano, but he was in love with Marsha. The problem was, Marsha was in love with a few other guys too.

They would not bother to head home when they closed the club down; they'd just go to another late, late club and wait for the 2:00 a.m. crowd to arrive. People would drive all the way from Houston to listen to these young musicians jam. He realized that playing with the older guys a few nights a week was better than a year in college.

Once when things were quiet, and people were taking a break, he'd go to the Whirlitzer, and dropped a half dozen quarters in and he'd dance with Sydney for a while; then she'd want to listen and drink her vodka (she'd always bring her own, as we all did, since it was "dry" in Texas in those days).

They were free as birds, and really young kids, but seldom thought about tomorrow. Invisible to the unknowing; with dreams of something they knew was bigger, but not more fun. Couldn't be. He'd always heard that when you find your love, stay with it, no matter what else comes. Maybe he figured this was what the poets called happiness.

Anyway, he finally would be able to dance with Marsha. She'd always play Judy Garland or Dinah Washington and he would notice her hair, long and blonde, always needing a little more peroxide or whatever they used to make her the most desirable thing he had seen in his short life. She'd wear knit dresses and soft sweaters and when they danced close he'd remember that while Marsha was 18, the experienced musicians would always tell him the problems of getting serious with a Singer. But hell, what did they know?

Although he made good grades, his life was destined to switch songs in the middle of the gig. He got his military draft call on a cold, drizzling January day and figured he'd go ahead and join the Marines; he thought for sure he'd play in the band. It didn't work quite like he planned; but that's another tale, for another time...three years best forgotten.

Now, back from Korea, he took up the horn again. And later, while working in Austin, he saw Sydney. She was at a steak house there and she told him she'd just married Bill Anthony, who was the executive producer of *Austin City Lights*. He thought, "How appropriate—What a fit!"

He later heard they were divorced.

One evening in his room in Austin, after starting grad school, he recalled that in those short early days of undergraduate times, one of his musician pals dated Marsha and he Sydney. They'd double and rather than the movies, they'd go to the old joints and listen to the same music that always made folks smile. The young man always kept his tenor in his car trunk, which allowed him to sit in with the band and play. Then after they took the girls home, and he dropped his pal off, he'd go back and pick up Marsha. And apparently, no one knew the difference even though the sisters lived in the same house. He'd only met their parents twice. Even then, pulling this off was a tough trip; however, the intrigue and assumed secrecy was something he never spoke of and never tried to forget. There's magic available when you're young.

He never asked how she got in and out without her sister knowing it. (Maybe she didn't.)

Those times were good.

He lost track of both sisters after he went back to graduate school. But he could never forget how those two could make music. They could have been great.

And now, when he recalled that soft familiar voice, and listened to a singer on a jazz radio station, he would wonder about Marsha.

Funny thing. That night in Austin nearly 40 years ago, he forgot to ask Sydney about Marsha.

Paige Planchard
October 25, 1996, Delta Flight 16, Atlanta

*I*f he had had the altitude and the eyes, he could look to his right, out of the plane's window and see the Big Easy...even through the dark rain.

He wondered where Paige Planchard was.

He had met her in a perfume shop in New Orleans in 1966 and was totally captivated. She was very tall, dressed in all black and "fit in" in New Orleans back in 1966...she carried perfect eye shadow, her lipstick was heavy and "off base"...like Gloria Graham's in old black and white movies with John Garfield...or the current young one, Jennifer Tilley...

He had little money, but he did have an officer's uniform (Navy). He had taken his basketball team to New Orleans and had put them to bed before heading to the French Quarter. His first trip. He'd had it made...great peacetime civilian Navy job in Pensacola, and another paid-for trip. He'd known a few of those in his 23 years.

Paige was a beautiful woman. He had no idea what her age was, but he did know that she was older than he. After Paige ordered drinks

Caliche Dust

from a bar next door, and served him, she said: "Cheers!...time I closed anyway! Wanna go see the French Quarter?"

Paige showed him all of it. There were quiet bars with old men playing Dixieland and boisterous ones where they alone were white. They listened to the jazz and drank bourbon on her tab. As he recalled, the bar lighting was just perfect. He could see the sweat beads on the trumpet player's face. The singer, her name was Ella. She sang the blues with a sad sounding vibrato. He also saw where sweat had caused a wisp of dark hair to help frame her face which was the color of creamed coffee.

After more drinks they moved outside. They talked of his work and her shop and had more drinks as they walked the narrow French Quarter streets. Her body was warm and he pulled her closer to him as they stopped to listen to the clarinet player on the street play for money pitched into his horn case.

He noticed it was as hot on the crowded street as it was inside; and in every new joint they floated to, the lead musician's eyes were closed behind dark glasses. The young Ensign had been around enough to know that the glasses served to hide the eyes of the wearer, which showed the evidence of snorting something other than powdered sugar.

None of the barroom's doors were closed; they had left the doors open to help keep the joint cool. Every club had its doors open and the music came together in an unusually strange mixed jazz way so that he couldn't place its origin. It was better than anything he had heard before. The sound that hit the street with a smiling beat, seemed like solid happiness.

After more drinks and a short cab ride, they both knew where they were going. She led him up the stairs to her apartment.

Her place had the highest ceiling he'd ever seen. Even the couch was French New Orleans. They sat, smoked Chesterfields and shared a grey colored drink in a small glass... absinthe? This stuff was more than just alcohol. He chuckled when he remembered a sign that he saw once:

"Absinthe makes the heart grow fonder."

Much later she spoke of her time in Cuba, before Castro. As a young girl she worked in Batista's government and fled to Miami with two other women during the revolution. She had stopped in Florida only a short time—said she knew the Big Easy was calling.

The Perfume Shop belonged to her, he figured, since the apartment was expensively decorated. But he found out over breakfast that she was being kept by a very wealthy guy... and the Perfume Shop was his idea, and he was the owner.

Years later the young Ensign would go back to the Perfume Shop. It, like Paige, was no longer there. But he'd remember that first night they'd met. She was the most mature lady he'd had. It was an evening he'd not be able to forget—nor did he try. He knew he'd always remember the quiet rain and a soft breeze that stirred both of them from sleep to again make love. Afterwards he'd seen a tear go down her cheek. All he could figure was for some reason this was a sad time for her. However, something swept over him that said he would never see her again.

But still he looked. Once, on another trip into the Quarter, months later, he thought he'd seen her in a bar...the Carousel. This brought back that night when they were stuck under an awning in the Quarter and she kissed him—in the rain...he saw again the raindrops on her cheeks which is why the mascara ran, he guessed. The puzzled young Naval Officer reckoned it had never happened to him before like this. Sure, Paige was different—hell, she was a mature lady like none had ever crossed his path before.

The kiss told him everything. After all, it was easy to see that he was much younger. And this made them both sad.

This was not the first time she had tried to retreat from the trap she had been in for too many years. The true touch of closeness the young officer possessed was heartbreakingly sweet and at the same time defeating. Standing there watching the rain drill the sidewalk lit by the flickering streetlight, he saw all those past years of mistakes disappear and she was aware that the trap had been sprung—she was caught—not the first but the last time—no escape—not enough time. So she stepped from under the awning, dabbed at her mascara and kissed him goodbye.

As he became older, and on wind swept nights, the once young officer wonders about Paige Planchard.

Caliche Dust

He remembered her at 19... maybe 20.
He'd walked that day in the caliche dust
and the heat of the South Texas sun to the
place where they would meet in town.

He was 21 and she wore the tan of her body
like a torch singer's gown...
no hose... slight heels...
and defying the mores of the small town...
she wore the dress short...
They would know each other for the next
three years and would fall deeply
In love...

They would go their own way...
to do the things expected of them...

And so they lost track...
as always happens...
when young lovers make promises
too hard to keep.

In the small car at the airport...
years later...
They both figured they could
have made it...
But they had not... too late.
It had always been too late.

Then, after 40 years he finally saw her
again... at an airport...
in the rain...
And at dinner there was
that same something... real or imagined.

For a few hours they talked of
their lives and all of the things
old lovers speak of...

She'd told him she'd loved him
from the start... had never stopped.
But they did not speak of mistakes made
or
of the things which had passed of which
they no longer could control.

They spoke of their children...
and she wondered what theirs would have
accomplished
and he wondered (silently) how they would have looked
(probably tall)

They talked of Spain and the bright
hills where she would walk
and how she wished he could come there
(which she knew was impossible)

In a flashing instant he wished he
could divide himself (like a cell, he thought)
and go there with her.

But he had never been that way
...and she knew that

One year later... she had written him
that she had found someone...
who had loved her and she him...
closed book.
And once again... he reflected on all
the things that they had missed...
not talked about enough...

The first name he thought of was

Hemingway...

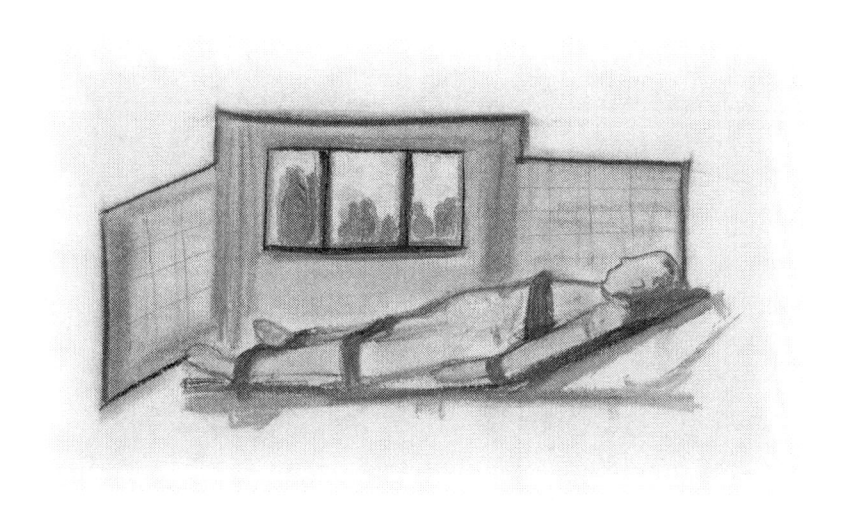

Keeping Quiet

Mick read on page 4 of the *Dallas Morning News* that Arthur Spencer Haynes was to be executed Tuesday night by lethal injection—smoother and easier than the kick from the sawed-off double barrel Artie had used on that rain washed night outside the Oui Bar, when Phil Jensen finally met his maker. But that's not the reason he got the chicken fried steak and side dishes that all condemned criminals request before their final set up. Haynes got the juice for another killing: Had something to do with a woman, one of his "employees." Louise, a dirty blonde who told one too many people about her "employer's" dope stash—he was caught with the gun in his hand. Hell, the DA had dropped the charges for killing Jensen well before this. There was nothing but circumstantial evidence in the Jensen case. But now the executioner would have his way—thanks to talkative Louise.

As Mick clipped the article, he moved back in his mind to the night nearly six years ago after Arti had suddenly told the whole story to Steve.

That was the time Haynes had stopped by Steve's pad to drop off some slacks and jackets. Haynes smilingly explained that they had "fallen off a truck" and Steve had called Mick to come by and see if some of them fit. According to Steve, Arti always felt comfortable to be at Steve's pad. Steve was, you see, single and had an unnoticeable apartment right next to a suburban library. He also booked a little football on the side. Anyway, after 4 or 5 drinks Arti reminded Steve that Phil Jensen had been killed last August and the case was still being worked. Suddenly, for no apparent reason, Artie blurted out the whole story; that he was the one who had hit Jensen. Thanks to three well-poured vodka martinis, he told Steve (almost like a confession) the bloody details.

Almost everybody knew that Jensen and Haynes had bad blood between them for years. They were both in the minor rackets: gambling, burglary, extortion, and whatever else could get you a long visit in the Huntsville Penitentiary.

And then there was a jewelry robbery involving some unique characters from Artie's old Dallas gang. Phil, who had recruited some of the Dallas gang, noticed that some contraband had been "missing." And because of their long untrusting personalities, Jensen was sure that Artie was behind the missing stash. Henson had bragged with some guys at a westside bar that he was going to kill Haynes. And of course Arti got wind of it and simply decided that he'd strike first.

So, eight days later...

"Where in the hell is Phil?" It was a long wait outside the Sundance Bar the night it happened; finished was a pack of Winstons and a six pack in Arti's front seat. Arti thought the guy must be planning to close the joint down. Finally, around 1:30 a.m., according to Arti, Jensen was alone when he eased through the heavy oak door and Artie told Steve how he had stumbled out of the car to finish Jensen off with a second round. He claimed it was easier than the first, since most of Jensen's upper torso was already gone. (Haynes had been accurate with the first blast from the driver's side front seat.) Steve said later that Artie continued with a long tale of how Jensen had it coming.

Ending his story, Arti told how he convinced the cops and the DA investigator that he had been with one of his "ladies" all night. And, closing his tale to Steve, he smiled at the memory. "No Steve, I was never scared; in fact I never slept better in my life."

Keeping Quiet

A few weeks later Steve and Mick heard the cops weren't working the case hard. And the DA's office was glad to be rid of a pretty tough outlaw with no trial to worry about.

Steve and Mick swore to each other that they would never tell anybody what Arti Haynes had confessed. They both realized they'd be pretty shaken in a murder trial. They both admittedly, were seriously scared. This was no longer shoplifting or burglaries, it was a gangland murder.

Two years later...

Mick was traveling to San Antonio/Houston Austin on a business trip. (He was in the softwear business.) He knew that he would be in Houston by Friday night. He had thought about the secret he and his pal harbored, at least once a week since that night in Fort Worth that Artie "confessed." To top it off he was still edgy and scared they would reopen the case. He couldn't forget the picture related by Steve of Jensen laying there in a pool of his own blood, with most of his upper body flowing into the gutter. He was giving it his best shot to walk away from that mind-stiring story.

In those days Coors beer was a very popular brand in Colorado and they had recently opened a distribution center in Fort Worth. Mick had stopped, picked up a case of Coors and put it in his ice chest to take to his old friend Bobby Doyle in Houston. Bobby was a blind white piano player. The only one Mick had ever met. Bobby ended up with the Fifth Edition for a while and then back to Houston. His singer was Joyce Webb, who later retired but continued to sing in small clubs and festivals in South Texas. Anyway, Mick had driven for what seemed hours to Houston from San Antonio. He got to the Houstonaire Motel where Bobby played, parked his car, and checked in. He went to the bar and saw Bobby was getting ready to take a break. Mick went up and hugged Bobby and passed him the Coors. Bobby had just cut a new CD and gave a copy to Mick. Mick ordered a drink, sat down at a table and began to unwind from his trip from San Antonio.

After making a few calls Mick noticed, sitting at a table nearby there were 3 guys having some drinks together and it looked like they were celebrating. They were pretty loose and there wasn't a crowd in the bar so they invited Mick over. Mick joined them and they began a conversation.

Caliche Dust

They were celebrating the birth of one of the guy's son. The man who had the son looked like he was close to 50 and was a pretty cool, tough looking guy. He introduced himself as Billy Sheets. Sheets said he owned a health club, and gave Mick his card. As the conversation continued, Sheets found out that Mick was from Fort Worth and they began playing "do you know...?" Both of them mentioned names, and finally Mick mentioned Theo Guilliam's name (he was an old gambler who would bet when a bird would fly off a limb). Then Billy Sheets said something that made Mick sit up tall.

"Yea, I know Theo and Puny. Hell, son, I was the biggest pimp in Richland Hills." Mick's eyes opened wide and before he knew what he was saying he questioned, "Well, did you know Arti Haynes?"

The answer totally floored Mick when Billy Sheets said "Oh, you mean the guy that killed Phil Jenson?" Mick blinked and swallowed hard. He knew that this could be a set up" and began to get the old sickness in his stomach. Happily Sheets ended the conversation with a nod and a smile. And later he introduced Mick to a couple of his friends that were dealers in dope (no secret there). Later on, Billy asked Mick if he had been to the Third Ward before and he said, "No." Mick thought that all the joints closed at 1:00 A.M. Maybe in Fort Worth, but not in Houston. Their quick trip to a club nearby soon proved that Houston was different.

Mick watched the late night crowd on the floor and began to wonder if these guys had real jobs. Hell, they all wore tuxes and the women wore one or two types of dresses—long or mini.

Billy Sheets and his two friends sat and drank and talked about basketball games and point spreads like some sort of code. Mick began to realize that he wasn't comfortable here. His two years of "straight life" was too good to let these guys mess it up.

Mick and Steve never told anyone that Haynes had killed Jensen. They had kept it a total secret, if for no other reason than to protect Arti Haynes' family and naturally to keep them off the witness list.

Sheets then turned to Mick and told him that if he ever had any problems in Houston to call the number on the card and he'd see that it would be handled. Interesting how friendships are made—especially after one party had just become a new father, and there was plenty of

J&B on hand and a long held secret would be walking out the door—never to be invited in again.

Mick had thought about his past. He and his pal, Steve, were still bothered by the business that Artie and Phil had led them into. And to top it off, Mick was still trying change his life. Now Mick could forget the picture produced in his own mind of Jenson lying there, in a pool of his own blood with most of his upper body flowing into the gutter. Time was kind to both Mick and Steve because they did not dwell on that night except after certain tequila shots sitting alone in very private and quiet places.

Time Well Spent

He remembered her tanned arms and legs and soft brown hair. Her name was Margaret.

He'd never forgotten her blue eyes and the seeping sadness that came from them when he told her on that hot, bright, late spring day that he was leaving for another job assignment that afternoon at 4:00.

For Lt. Melvin Wilson, recruited by the OSS, forerunner of the CIA, the 1950s furnished exciting times. Mel's "cover" was an export/import company based in the U.S. The job was one most young officers would kill for. Acting as a civilian rotating "sales agent," Mel would operate in various regions in North and sometimes Central America. The toughest part of his duty was accurately writing detailed reports on organized crime groups laundering money for Central American drug Cartels. Mel was fortunate, he was quite a talented writer and learned to write the kind of memos Foggy Bottom understood. It was also lucky that Mel had drawn a 4.0 GPA and spoke Spanish, Russian and Portuguese, thanks to a tough private school education.

Anyway, Margaret and Mel sat on a Virginia hillside near the girl's school she attended and he began to say goodbye. She had told him the story of her baby and how she missed the child she had left at Lena Pope Home in Fort Worth, Texas for adoption. She had recalled how she'd walked Hemphill Street in 1952, not four blocks from Mel's home on Travis. She, waiting to have the child someone else would hold, pray for, buy tricycles and bicycles, and finally a car for. And Mel, home during that Christmas Holiday, at least for a few days and not having much fun either. Somehow, after knowing her that summer Mel thought they would have gotten along, even with her pregnant with the child she'd never know. Hell, she barely knew the father.

She gave him a book of hers, *This is My Beloved*. Mel must have kept that thing for 20 years. Occasionally he would pull it off the shelf and read parts that he had marked and underlined. Strangely enough he'd only known her for a month or so, but during that time they talked of making love (they never did) and of seeing each other later when his job was finished. He couldn't tell her about his real job of course, but he knew from the beginning there was nothing that made permanent sense, at least for Mel. She had brought a fresh clean scene to his life which only months before was not pretty. His father had died in March and they buried him before Mel left Texas for what turned out to be his covert military duty. Somehow this girl made things sweetly calm and beautiful during this lonely time.

Mel had written a poem about the hillside where they'd sat and talked about the future. And he had told her he thought he was in love with her. That's what happens when you're young and do not possess enough judgment to not burn bridges carefully. Mel still had his life ahead of him; and over the years, on special spring afternoons, he would wonder where this road he didn't take would have led him. Over the years he would discover that "Never Look Back" is a good piece of advice. Time is a marvelous healer—but it's a tough job to heal falling in love with what could have been the right one. Then there were other things: when you spend years at a job that becomes a trap and you're alone, and the higher up you move, the more valuable you become and finally you've figured out it is too late. He often wondered if the CIA wasn't the Mafia in disguise.

It was too soon for her, that year they had met. There were times when he wondered if it was as tough giving up her child for adoption as it was for him to board another plane—saying goodbye to no one. In other years, and in other cities, usually during Christmas season, Mel would think of her and hoped that she'd be able to have another child at the right time and with the right guy.

But what could he have done? There were times, when just before falling asleep, her wet, blue eyes came to him and holding her hand to her mouth, she'd smile and send a message that he could never understand.

In his September years, the now middle-aged CIA asset would occasionally wonder, after many other "no commitment" romantic encounters, why his mind always took him back to that Virginia hillside. Maybe she'd taken as much from him as he had from her.

At times like this he would sadly remember an old country love song's lyric which went, "Quietly she'd ease through my mind...She was one of a kind..."

Goodbye
(What's good about Goodbye?)

He wondered if she was still in Spain or had she given up the cabin there on the high ridge bathed by the sun, warming the hills where she had walked and where she had thought of Him back in the city. He often wished now that He had gone to her, for at least a short time.

Maybe she had decided to go back to the caliche streets in the South Texas town where no one ever discussed global warming—not even considered it—should not even ask. He remembered the hot South Texas days when there was no wind and when a truck rolled down one of those streets; the caliche dust would rise and hang like a ghostly white thunder cloud.

The sun in that town was not like that in Spain. She'd gone to England once because she'd always heard you had to do the things about which all the others asked. Somehow that never worked out, except for Him and He always ended as a dream in which she never had the chance to do the beautiful things she had wanted to do with Him—and He realized that He would rather think of her in Spain where Heming-

Caliche Dust

way had lived and written. London and the Thames never seemed to fit with her style—leather sandals and white shirts with perfectly faded jeans. He had seen her for the first time and was certain her hips would always be lean and lovely.

He mused on the irony of this—she in Spain and he in Austin, where they had quietly in a mystical way, sat and felt the earth with their fingers , and later made love in the cabin, talking again of the beach and the sand sticking to their bodies. And later (in their thoughts) made love in the cabin, and raised the curtain on the window's opening, sucking in the air with dry mouths; the same air that Hemingway had tasted. And later the wine they brought from the rental car (they both would rather have Scotch) and with wetted bodies they slept for only a short time—then later he remembered the night in the Italian place when they drank the wine and sat in a large booth so that he was very close with his leg behind her and his hand resting on warm, thin cotton cloth. Here they talked of all the old times, of the days in Austin and the private, quiet times in that club on Saturday afternoons up on US 81, during football games which neither cared for. And how with only a few couples in booths along the wall they would dance to the DeCastro Sisters' harmony, kiss leaning on a table, and vow their forever love at least (for her) even after she finished college (and he) even after he was free from his obligations (he knew of course, that would never happen).

So now a half century later, he still wished he could divide himself. He once had written "like a cell" and find her once more.

He'd start on that slow train from Houston and only find that once-caliche-dust road in South Texas was now paved asphalt. Probably no one would even remember her name—besides now he was too old to begin the task. He'd heard the little town was now no longer little. All the old men were now gone, or buried, or in a nursing home telling their grown children confusing lies that become truer the more they are told.

But he once again saw her in his mind: tall, tanned, weepingly beautiful, still smiling, wearing that white pleated skirt that lay lovingly on her legs when she walked; still with those sad brown eyes.

Now he said goodbye forever. Only this time she didn't respond.

Made in the USA
Charleston, SC
08 June 2015